'ROUND and AROUND

'ROUND and AROUND

by James Skofield

illustrated by James Graham Hale

HarperCollins*Publishers*

Library of Congress Cataloging-in-Publication Data
Skofield, James.
    'Round and around / by James Skofield ; illustrated by James
Graham Hale.
        p.   cm.
    Summary: A little boy and his father go for a walk and find circular
shapes in everything they see and do.
        ISBN 0-06-025746-6. — ISBN 0-06-025747-4 (lib. bdg.)
    [1. Circle—Fiction.   2. Fathers and sons—Fiction.]   I. Hale, James
Graham, ill.   II. Title.
PZ7.S62835Ro   1993   90-32831
[E]—dc20   CIP
                                                        AC

Typography by Christine Kettner
1   2   3   4   5   6   7   8   9   10
❖
First Edition

for Glenn

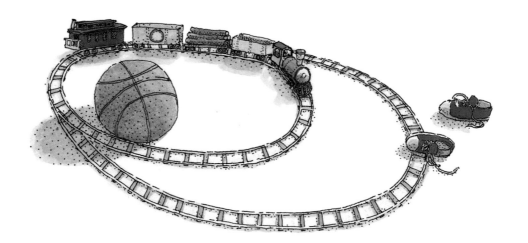

It was after supper and Dan and his dad and their dog, Sam, were taking a walk in the cool spring air. They felt the roadside gravel crunch under their feet. They listened to the evening wind talking in the trees. They watched the round red sun sink behind the fields.

"Why does the sun go down?" Dan asked.

His dad lifted him over the fence and set him down on a tree stump. "Well," he began, "when the Earth makes a circle around the sun . . ."

"A circle is round," said Dan.

"That's right," said his dad. "It has no beginning; it has no end."

Away down the path, Sam barked. Seconds later, a gray-brown rabbit came streaking past with Sam right behind. Out over the field the animals raced, in huge round circles.

"Yo, Sam!" Dan's dad called sharply. He whistled, and Sam broke off from the chase and trotted back. His red tongue lolled and his black eyes snapped. "That's enough out of *you*," said Dan's dad.

"The rabbit and Sam ran in circles," Dan said. "'Round and around and around."

"So they did," said his dad. "'Round and around and around."

"This tree stump has circles," said Dan to his dad. "Circles in circles in circles."

"Trees make circles as they grow: one circle for each year."

High up above, a golden hawk hunted, circling silently over the fields.

"I wish I could fly," Dan said to his dad.

"Let's see if you can," his dad answered. He grabbed hold of Dan's wrists and he swung him . . . 'round and around and around until the world was a dizzy, laughing, blurring circle. When the world stopped spinning, Dan leaned on his dad, and after a while they went on.

The dusky woods were dark and cool. Somewhere deep inside the shadows, two owls hooted back and forth.

Dan and his dad sat down on a rock beside a small, round pool. Sam sighed and turned around three times and settled at their feet. Dan pitched pebbles into the water and watched ripples spread in circles on the surface. His dad took out his tobacco and pipe and puffed smoke rings up into the air.

Together, they listened to the tree frogs and watched the first, far, ice-blue stars wink on in the evening sky.

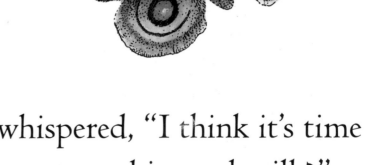

After a time, Dan's dad whispered, "I think it's time we were home. How about some cookies and milk?"

Dan and his dad sat in the kitchen. The lamp made a circle of light on the ceiling. The cookies had raisins. The milk was cold.

Dan dipped his finger in the milk and rubbed it around the rim of the glass. Around and around the top of the glass until the wet glass squeaked.

"Now drink your milk," said Dan's dad. So Dan drank his milk and ate his cookie.

"Bath time," said Dan's dad.

"Catch me first," said Dan.

So Dan's dad chased Dan around the table . . . 'round and around and around. He caught him and teased him and tickled him, and then he circled his arms around his little boy and hugged him.

"A hug is a circle, too," he said softly and he carried him up the stairs to the bath. Sam followed at his heels.

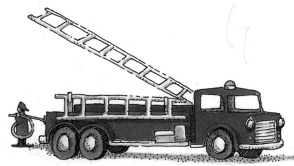

Dan and his dad soaked together in the hot water. They laughed and poked each other's belly buttons. Dan's dad washed Dan's hair and dunked him. Then Dan washed his dad's hair and dunked *him*. They toweled each other dry and got into their pajamas. The buttons on their pajamas made a row of circles right up their fronts.

Dan's dad carried Dan into his bedroom. He tucked Dan in and kissed him good-night.

"But *why* does the sun go down?" Dan asked.

His dad sat down on the edge of the bed.

"When the sun goes down, it is rising on the other side of the world," he said. "And there, another little boy is waking up to play. When we have night, he has day. So night and day chase 'round the world. 'Round and around and around. And now it's time to sleep. Good night."

Dan's dad went out and shut the door. Soon he was asleep in his own warm bed and the house was still and dark.

But Dan got out of bed and walked to his window. He leaned his arms on the windowsill and he watched the round, white moon rise up.

"The world goes 'round," whispered Dan to Sam. "'Round and around and around. . . ."

JAMES SKOFIELD is the author of several books for children, including NIGHT-DANCES, SNOW COUNTRY, and ALL WET! ALL WET!, an NSTA/CBC Outstanding Science Book of 1984. He is also a translator of French and German. His translations include four books by the German author Irina Korschunow: THE FOUNDLING FOX, ADAM DRAWS HIMSELF A DRAGON, SMALL FUR, and SMALL FUR IS GETTING BIGGER. Mr. Skofield lives and writes in New York City.

JAMES GRAHAM HALE has illustrated two other books for children: Ann Turner's THROUGH MOON AND STARS AND NIGHT SKIES, a Reading Rainbow Featured Selection, and WHO'S GOING TO TAKE CARE OF ME? by Michelle Magorian. Mr. Hale was born and grew up in Ohio, was graduated from Denison University, and currently lives in Ulster Park, New York.